PEAS
IN A POD

ADÈLE GERAS

Illustrated by Peter Bailey

For Sophie and Stephanie Pitt

PEAS IN A POD
A CORGI BOOK 978 0 552 56895 1

Published in Great Britain by Corgi Books,
an imprint of Random House Children's Publishers UK
A Random House Group Company

Corgi Pups edition published 2000
This Colour First Reader edition published 2013

1 3 5 7 9 10 8 6 4 2

Copyright © Adèle Geras, 2000
Illustrations copyright © Peter Bailey, 2000

The Random House Group Limited supports the Forest Stewardship Council (FSC®),
the leading international forest certification organization. Our books carrying the FSC
label are printed on FSC®-certified paper. FSC is the only forest certification scheme
endorsed by the leading environmental organizations, including Greenpeace. Our paper
procurement policy can be found at www.randomhouse.co.uk/environment.

Set in Bembo MT Schoolbook 21/28pt

Corgi Books are published by Random House Children's Publishers UK,
61–63 Uxbridge Road, London W5 5SA

www.**randomhousechildrens**.co.uk
www.**randomhouse**.co.uk

Addresses for companies within The Random House Group Limited can be found at:
www.randomhouse.co.uk/offices.htm

THE RANDOM HOUSE GROUP Limited Reg. No. 954009

A CIP catalogue record for this book is available from the British Library.

Printed in Italy.

Contents

Series Reading Consultant: Prue Goodwin
Honorary Fellow of the University of Reading

Chapter One

When Stella-across-the-road decided to get married, Jo was very happy. "I bet she asks us to be her bridesmaids," she told her sister Lily.

"She's been our babysitter for years and years, so we're practically family. We'll have really beautiful clothes to wear. I can't wait."

Lily sniffed, and didn't look happy at all. "I don't want to be a bridesmaid. Maybe she'll decide she only wants one bridesmaid, and then she's sure to choose you."

Jo was nine years old. She was small and thin. Lily was seven and tall for her age. Sometimes, when they were dressed alike, people thought they might be twins, and this made Jo cross,

because she hated
being the same
size as someone
who was two
years younger.
Lily hated putting
on dresses or
skirts and spent
most of her time wearing jeans.

Jo wanted to be a
ballerina when she
grew up but, for
the moment, being
a bridesmaid was
one of her main
ambitions.

Michelle, her friend, had been
one last year, and Jo felt very
envious. Now maybe her dream
was going to come true.

Jo drew pictures of pretty bridesmaids on every spare piece of paper she could find. Some had ribbons in their hair, some had flowers all over their dresses, but all the skirts were long and puffed-out. Jo thought they were lovely.

Sometimes she made Lily play weddings. "You can be the groom," she said. "I'll be the bride."

Lily quite enjoyed being the groom, because she didn't have to change out of her jeans.

Every night in bed Jo said: "I wonder why Stella is taking such ages to ask us to be bridesmaids."

"I don't know," said Lily.
"Don't worry about it. Go to sleep."

But Jo did worry about it.

The next day she made Lily play hopscotch with her outside Stella's house.

"Hello, girls," said Stella when she came down the road on her way back from work. "Are you looking forward to my wedding? I've got to write the invitations tonight." She went in without saying a word about bridesmaids.

"We'll come back again tomorrow," Jo said. "If she keeps seeing us, she'll remember in the end that she hasn't asked us yet."

After two weeks of hanging about outside Stella's house, Lily and Jo gave up. Stella's mum, Mrs Grainger, had chatted to them about flower arrangements; Stella's granny had asked them in for a drink and a biscuit, and shown them a picture of what the wedding cake was going

to look like. No-one had even
mentioned bridesmaids.

"Maybe," said Lily, "she's not
going to have any."

That was such an awful thing
to say that Jo decided to pretend
that she hadn't heard it.

Chapter Two

Then one day Stella's mum came in to have a cup of coffee with Lily and Jo's mum. "Wedding day's nearly here," she said. "Aren't you getting excited, girls?"

Jo opened her mouth to ask about the bridesmaids, but Mrs Grainger just kept on talking.

"It's going to be a wedding to remember," she told them. "Three bridesmaids and two pages – that's Stella's cousins and her niece and nephews – and the best man and me and Stella's dad and granny.

It's going to be quite a crowd but just wait till you hear where they're having the wedding – in the Rose Garden at Hatton Hall. You know, that stately home just outside town. Stella's gran thinks it's a shame not to have a wedding in a church, or at least a Registry Office, but everyone has to do what will make them happy. That's what I think."

Lily was just going to ask what happened if it rained, when Mrs Grainger said, as though she had been reading Lily's mind: "And if it rains, there's a lovely big drawing room they use for the weddings."

Jo wasn't really listening. She was too upset. She wasn't going to be a bridesmaid after all. It isn't fair, she said to herself.

She blinked very quickly, because she felt like crying, but she was going to wait till she and Lily were alone to do that. This was easily the saddest day of her whole life.

After Mrs Grainger had
finished telling them how grand
the wedding was going to be, she
said goodbye and went home.

"I hope it pours with rain!" Jo
shouted after her. "I hope they
have a horrible wedding. I hope
the wedding cake tastes awful!"

"Jo!" said Mum. "What's the matter with you? Why are you behaving like a little monster?"

"She thought we were going to be bridesmaids," Lily explained. "And we're not, so now she's fed up. I'm not fed up. I'm glad."

"Then you're a silly little brat!"
Jo shouted and left the room in
a temper, slamming the door
behind her.

"Oh dear," said Mum. "I was just about to tell her that I'm going to buy lovely dresses for you both to wear. I'll go after her and try to cheer her up." She ran upstairs after Jo.

It was Lily's turn to look glum. She didn't want a lovely

dress. She wanted a new pair of trainers with silver stripes on them.

Chapter Three

On the morning
of Stella's
wedding day
Jo was ready
straight after
breakfast, but

Lily was taking ages
to put on last year's
party frock. She'd
refused to wear
anything like Jo's
new dress.

"Come on, Lily!" Jo called out.
"It's time to go over now and
see Stella's dress and meet the
bridesmaids."

She looked out of the window.

The sun was trying to shine, but
clouds were rushing across the
sky, and sometimes they became
dark and heavy and rain started
falling, blown about by a strong
wind. She wondered if she had
made the bad weather appear
by wishing for it. Maybe Stella

would have to get married
indoors after all. Her veil would
be blown about all over the
place. The hem of her dress and
her train might drag in a puddle
and get it all muddy.

"Right," said Lily, coming into the room. "I'm ready now."

"We're going then, Mum," said Jo. "Is that OK?"

"Be back here by half past," said Mum. "We're getting a lift down to Hatton Hall with Stella's Uncle Archie. Just wait for this shower to be over."

"Why are you still looking cross?" Lily asked Jo. "I'm the one who should be cross. I hate this dress. I look stupid. You like yours, I know you do."

Jo didn't answer straight away. She *did* like her dress, which was lilac and lacy with a wide velvet sash for a belt. Mum had bought a special matching velvet ribbon for her hair. She knew she looked pretty, but still . . .

"I wanted to go in a shiny car," she said to Lily. "And the bridesmaids have got baskets to carry. With real flowers in them."

"Stella's got to choose her relations first," Lily said.

"I know," said Jo, "but she could have had us as well."

"Then the whole garden would be full of bridesmaids," said Lily. "It'd look silly."

"It wouldn't," said Jo.

"Would," said Lily.

"Stop squabbling, girls," said Mum, "and go across the road. It's very kind of the Graingers to invite you. They must be run off their feet."

The Graingers' house was so full of people that Lily and Jo could hardly find a corner to stand in. Stella's granny was trying to see herself in the  hall mirror, Mrs Grainger was

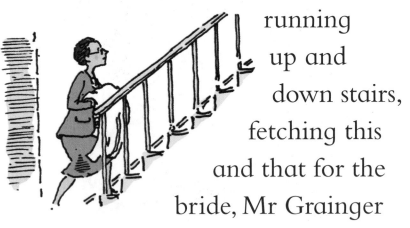 running up and down stairs, fetching this and that for the bride, Mr Grainger was mumbling in the kitchen,

 practising his
speech, and Pepper,
Stella's little brown
and white dog, was
racing from room
to room. Every now and then
he stopped in the
middle of the carpet
and began chasing
his own tail.

"Come with me, girls," said
Mrs Grainger. She
was already dressed
for the wedding,
but still had rollers
in her hair.

"What if she forgets?" Lily asked Jo in a whisper. "Imagine how funny that'd be!"

"Ssh," said Jo. "She'll hear you."

Mrs Grainger opened Stella's bedroom door and Lily and Jo went in.

"Oooh!" said Jo. She wanted to say so many things, and couldn't think of one of them. Stella looked just like a princess. Her hair was done up in an enormous

heap of curls on top of her head.
Her dress was made of satin. There
were tiny pearls scattered all over
the bodice in flower patterns.

"You look beautiful," said Lily.
"Really, truly beautiful."

"I was going to say that," said
Jo crossly.

Stella smiled at them both.
"So do you," she said,
and then she made a
funny face, pretending
to be scared. "But
I'm feeling a bit
nervous. Something's
bound to go
wrong."

"No it won't,"
said Jo. "everything will be
perfect."

"Now, Lily and Jo," said
Stella. "I'd like you to meet my
bridesmaids – Ruthie, Bridie and
Little Amee."

"Hello," said Lily.

"Hello," said Jo.

"Hello," said Ruthie, who was
the eldest. "We've been told to sit
as quiet as mice, and not move,
in case our dresses get dirty."

The bridesmaids were wearing
pale blue silky dresses.

They had white rosebuds
pinned into their hair. Jo was just
thinking how lovely they looked
and feeling sad all over again at
not being a bridesmaid, when
they heard it. Mrs Grainger was
shrieking in the hall. What on
earth had happened?

Chapter Four

Jo and Lily ran downstairs.
Stella's mum was standing by the
front door talking to her
daughter-in-law Margie
who was all dressed up in
her wedding clothes.

"Why didn't you tell me
earlier?" she wailed. "I could have
done something. And what about
poor little Matt and Peter? Who's
going to look after them? Your
next-door neighbour? Well, I don't
know what to say, I really don't."

"Come on now, dearest," said Mr Grainger. "What's the problem?"

"Those two scallywags have only chosen today to break out in German measles, that's what," said Stella's mum.

"And here's Margie with their clothes in a parcel. As if I could find two pages at a moment's notice! I ask you!"

"I must go," said Margie. "I promised the boys I'd get out a DVD for them before we leave for the wedding." She was gone, and Mr Grainger closed the door behind her.

By now, even Stella had come to see what was going on. "Let's go and sit down," she said. "There's nothing to worry about. I've got three bridesmaids after all."

"I spent a fortune on those pages' suits," Mrs Grainger sniffed. "What a waste!"

"Two pairs of blue velvet trousers," said Stella, laying them carefully on the back of the sofa. "Two white silk shirts. Two pairs of black shoes with silver buckles. And two gorgeous silver brocade waistcoats."

The Grainger family gathered around the sofa and sighed over the clothes. Granny Grainger put her glasses on and stared at Lily and Jo. "I've had an idea," she said.

"Later, Mother, dear," said Mrs

Grainger. "You can tell us later.
We've got to get going now. The
cars will be here in half an hour."

"Later will be too late," said
Granny Grainger. "I've solved
the problem. I've found you two
pages."

"Where?" said Stella, and all
the Graingers looked around
as though pages might have
been hiding somewhere in their
lounge.

Granny Grainger pointed at Lily and Jo. "There," she said.

"But they're girls, Granny," said Stella. "How can you have girl pages?"

"I don't see why not. Don't call them pages, that's all. Call them . . . I don't know . . . attendants. That's it. Wedding attendants."

Everyone was quiet for a moment, then Stella said, "It might work . . . what do you think, Lily? And you, Jo? I never

realized how alike you two were. Just like two peas in a pod, you'd be, if you wore matching suits. How do you feel about standing in for the boys? You're very important, you know. You have to carry the bridal train. Do you think you could manage that?"

 "Oh, yes," said Jo. "But will the clothes fit us?"

"Nothing a safety pin or two won't be able to fix," said Granny.

"Go and try them on," said Mrs Grainger, "while I run across and warn your mum that you might be coming with us in the wedding party."

Chapter Five

Lily and Jo stared at their reflections in Stella's long mirror.

"Well," said Mrs Grainger. "A bit of a rush job but, though I say it myself, you both look wonderful."

"Brilliant!" Lily agreed. "I pretend to be a boy all the time

anyway, so I'm really good at it. People might think I'm a real boy, mightn't they?"

"Course they won't," said Jo. "You've got girls' black shoes on, haven't you?"

"It doesn't matter at all," said Stella. "We're lucky that the shoes were the only things that didn't really fit."

Jo didn't know if she was pleased or not. She would be riding in a shiny car. She would have her photo in the wedding

album. She and Lily would be
Very Important and everyone
would look at them, and say
how good it was of them to be

wedding attendants at the very
last minute. All that was going to
be like a dream come true, but
there was a tiny part of Jo that
was sorry she'd had to take off
her own lovely pink dress and
scrape her hair back into a tight
bun, and leave her velvet hair
ribbon at home.

And however smart she and
Lily looked, they still wouldn't
have long skirts, and baskets full of
flowers to carry. Jo and Lily were in
the second car, with Mrs Grainger
and Granny Grainger. It was shiny,
but not as big as the bride's car.
That was dark blue and there were
white ribbons tied to the bonnet,
and lots of white flowers
piled up against
the back

window. Stella
and her dad were
going to the wedding in it,
and so were the bridesmaids.

The rain was coming down
very heavily. Stella came out of
the front door with her satin skirt
pulled up so that it didn't get
wet and dirty. Mr Grainger was
holding an umbrella over her
and looking worried.

It was quite a long ride to
Hatton Hall. The rain splashed
against the windscreen. Jo
whispered to Lily: "It's my fault."

"What is?"
"This
rain," Jo said.
"Don't you
remember? I wished Stella would
have a rainy wedding day. Now
we'll have to be indoors."

"That's stupid," said Lily. "It's
not raining because you wished
it. And anyway, it's stopped.
Look."

There wasn't time to look.

They had arrived. Stella was
standing on the steps of the Hall,
looking like a white flower. There
was her groom and the best man,
and Ruthie, Bridie and Amee,
holding tight to their baskets of
white flowers. Lily and Jo went
up the steps and the
best man showed
them where they
had to stand.

"These," Stella said to everyone, "are my wedding attendants. They've taken over from Matt and Peter at very short notice. They're both real stars. Thank you, Jo and Lily!"

"You look brilliant," Ruthie whispered. "And you've got something proper to do, holding up Stella's train. We can't do anything with these flowers to carry."

"But won't the hem of the dress get muddy?" Jo asked.

"No," Bridie said. "They've put down a red carpet. Look."

Mrs Grainger showed Lily and Jo how to hold the train, and everyone set off for the Rose Garden, where all the guests were waiting for Stella and her bridesmaids to arrive.

"There are the pages," someone said. "They look quite splendid, don't they?"

Everyone clapped. Jo whispered to Lily: "I like being a wedding attendant. I don't even  mind not having a basket of flowers."

The sun shone down and made everything sparkle. Lily pulled her shoulders back and walked carefully along the red carpet, and Jo smiled at her, feeling happy that she was part of such a special wedding day.

THE END

Colour First Readers

Welcome to Colour First Readers. The following pages are intended for any adults (parents, relatives, teachers) who may buy these books to share the stories with youngsters. The pages explain a little about the different stages of learning to read and offer some suggestions about how best to support children at a very important point in their reading development.

Children start to learn about reading as soon as someone reads a book aloud to them when they are babies. Book-loving babies grow into toddlers who enjoy sitting on a lap listening to a story, looking at pictures or joining in with familiar words. Young children who have listened to stories start school with an expectation of enjoyment from books and this positive outlook helps as they are taught to read in the more formal context of school.

Cracking the code

Before they can enjoy reading for and to themselves, all children have to learn how to crack the alphabetic code and make meaning out of the lines and squiggles we call letters and punctuation. Some lucky pupils find the process of learning to read undemanding; some find it very hard.

Most children, within two or three years, become confident at working out what is written on the page. During this time they will probably read collections of books which are graded; that is, the books introduce a few new words and increase in length, thus helping youngsters gradually to build up their growing ability to work out the words and understand basic meanings.

Eventually, children will reach a crucial point when, without any extra help, they can decode words in an entire book, albeit a short one. They then enter the next phase of becoming a reader.

Making meaning

It is essential, at this point, that children stop seeing progress as gradually 'climbing a ladder' of books of ever-increasing difficulty. There is a transition stage between building word recognition skills and enjoying reading a story. Up until now, success has depended on getting the words right but to get pleasure from reading to themselves, children need to fully comprehend the content of what they read. Comprehension will only be reached if focus is put on understanding meaning and that can only happen if the reader is not hesitant when decoding. At this fragile, transition stage, decoding should be so easy that it slowly becomes automatic. Reading a book with ease enables children to get lost in the story, to enjoy the unfolding narrative at the same time as perfecting their newly learned word recognition skills.

At this stage in their reading development, children need to:

- Practice their newly established early decoding skills at a level which eventually enables them to do it automatically

- Concentrate on making sensible meanings from the words they decode

- Develop their ability to understand when meanings are 'between the lines' and other use of literary language

- Be introduced, very gradually, to longer books in order to build up stamina as readers

In other words, new readers need books that are well within their reading ability and that offer easy encounters with humour, inference, plot-twists etc. In the past, there have been very few children's books that provided children with these vital experiences at an early stage. Indeed, some children had to leap from highly controlled teaching materials to junior novels.

This experience often led to reluctance in youngsters who were not yet confident enough to tackle longer books.

Matching the books to reading development

Colour First Readers fill the gap between early reading and children's literature and, in doing so, support inexperienced readers at a vital time in their reading development. Reading aloud to children continues to be very important even after children have learned to read and, as they are well written by popular children's authors, Colour First Readers are great to read aloud. The stories provide plenty of opportunities for adults to demonstrate different voices or expression and, in a short time, give lots to talk about and enjoy together.

Each book in the series combines a number of highly beneficial features, including:

- Well-written and enjoyable stories by popular children's authors

- Unthreatening amounts of print on a page

- Unrestricted but accessible vocabularies

- A wide interest age to suit the different ages at which children might reach the transition stage of reading development

- Different sorts of stories – traditional, set in the past, present or future, real life and fantasy, comic and serious, adventures, mysteries etc.

- A range of engaging illustrations by different illustrators

- Stories which are as good to read aloud to children as they are to be read alone

All in all, Colour First Readers are to be welcomed for children throughout the early primary school years – not only for learning to read but also as a series of good stories to be shared by everyone. I like to think that the word 'Readers' in the title of this series refers to the many young children who will enjoy these books on their journey to becoming lifelong bookworms.

Prue Goodwin
Honorary Fellow of the University of Reading

Helping children to enjoy *Peas in a Pod*

If a child can read a page or two fluently, without struggling with the words at all, then he/she should be able to read this book alone. However, children are all different and need different levels of support to help them become confident enough to read a book to themselves.

Some young readers will not need any help to get going; they can just get on with enjoying the story. Others may lack confidence and need help getting into the story. For these children, it may help if you talk about what might happen in the book.

Explore the title, cover and first few illustrations with them, making comments and suggestions about any clues to what might happen in the story. Read the first chapter aloud together. Don't make it a chore. If they are still reluctant to do it alone, read the whole book with them, making it an enjoyable experience.

The following suggestions will not be necessary every time a book is read but, every so often, when a story has been particularly enjoyed, children love responding to it through creative activities.

Before reading

The title of this story, *Peas in a Pod*, may mean nothing to a child (other than a description of a vegetable) so it will be a good idea to talk about well-known sayings, explaining what they mean. The title comes from the simile, 'as alike as two peas in a pod,' although the two girls in the story are actually as different as chalk and cheese. As you start to read the book it will be easy to spot the differences between the girls. It will only be at the end that readers discover why *Peas in a Pod* is a good title.

During reading

Asking questions about a story can be really helpful to support understanding but don't ask too many – and don't make it feel like a test on what has happened. Relate the questions to the child's own experiences and imagination. For example, ask: 'Would you like to be a bridesmaid/page'; or 'Why do you think Lily and Jo haven't been invited to be bridesmaids?'

Responding to the book

If your child has enjoyed the story, it increases the fun by doing something creative in response. If possible, provide art materials and dressing up clothes so that they can make things, play at being characters, write and draw, act out a scene or respond imaginatively in some other way to the story.

Activities for children

If you have enjoyed reading this story, you could:

- Fill in the missing words in these sentences about the girls? Remember, Jo and Lily are sisters but they are very different. Chapter 1 may help you.

  - **Jo is the older sister so Lily is the _____ sister.**

  - **Jo likes to wear pretty _____ but Lily likes to wear _____.**

  - **Jo wants to be a _____ and one of her main ambitions is to be a _____.**

  - **Lily enjoys playing at being the groom because she can wear her _____.**

  - **_____ was disappointed about not being a bridesmaid but Lily didn't _____.**

- Look up weddings on the Internet. There are lots of ways that families celebrate when people get married and weddings are held in different places. Whatever happens, people always dress smartly and are very happy for the bride and groom. What would you choose to wear at a wedding? Design an outfit for yourself which will be smart, comfortable and make you feel happy.

- Get a pencil and piece of paper to do Stella-across-the-road's Wedding Quiz.

  1. Where did Stella's wedding take place? (Clue: page 22)

  2. How many bridesmaids were there? (Clue: page 21)

  3. Who should have been the two pages? (Clue: page 47)

  4. Who thought that Jo and Lily could be the pages? (Clue: pages 51 & 52)

  5. Why did Jo and Lily look like 'two peas in a pod' at the end of the story?

- Share the story with your friends and pretend you are having a wedding. Find something to dress up in so the bride has a long train to her dress.

ALSO AVAILABLE AS COLOUR FIRST READERS